The

CHRISTMAS WITCH

Story and pictures by

STEVEN KELLOGG

DIAL BOOKS FOR YOUNG READERS

New York

For LAURIE, 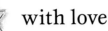 with love

Published by Dial Books for Young Readers
A Division of Penguin Books USA Inc.
375 Hudson Street / New York, New York 10014

Copyright © 1992 by Steven Kellogg
All rights reserved
Design by Jane Byers Bierhorst
Printed in the U.S.A.
First Edition
3 5 7 9 10 8 6 4

Library of Congress Cataloging in Publication Data

Kellogg, Steven.
The Christmas witch
story and pictures by Steven Kellogg. — 1st ed.
p.   cm.
Summary / Gloria must prove that she has what it
takes to become a Christmas Witch by bringing peace to a
planet occupied by two feuding factions.
ISBN 0-8037-1268-5 (trade). — ISBN 0-8037-1269-3 (library)
[1. Witches — Fiction.   2. Christmas — Fiction.] I. Title.
PZ7.K292Cj 1992 [E] — dc20 91-32688 CIP AC

The full-color artwork was prepared using ink and pencil line
and watercolor washes. It was then color-separated and
reproduced as red, blue, yellow, and black halftones.

Madame Pestilence expected her students at the Academy for Young Goblins and Witches to scowl at all times. It was one of the many rules that Gloria had trouble remembering.

Every time Madame Pestilence spotted Gloria passing her office, she would holler, "STOP SMILING!"

It was easy to scowl at dinnertime because the same awful creamed cockroach casserole was served every night. It made all of the students sick.

"Stop complaining!" Madame Pestilence would snarl. "This diet will turn you into wicked witches and goblins — as mean as your headmistress."

One evening at midnight the students were marched to broom drill. They chanted a chorus of magic phrases, and WHOOSH! WHOOSH! WHOOSH! The brooms snapped into take-off position and shot toward the moon.

One broom, however, refused to budge.

As usual Gloria had muddled the magic phrases. Madame Pestilence was furious. "Copy the first nine hundred and ninety-nine pages of the *Encyclopedia of Spells and Curses* nine hundred and ninety-nine times!" she screamed.

Madame Pestilence rocketed skyward, and Gloria was left alone.

Gloria was wearily at work on her assignment when suddenly she heard the tinkling of bells.

Following the sound, she went down a winding staircase and passed through a small doorway she'd never noticed before. There she discovered a storytelling circle where a stranger was reading a book called *A Magic Tale of Christmas*.

The story enchanted Gloria and filled her with joyful holiday visions. "I want to be a Christmas witch!" she cried.

"Christmas magic can bring about miracles," said Gloria's new friend. "But sometimes it takes courage and imagination to make Christmas wishes come true."

Summoning all the courage and imagination she could, Gloria cried, "I wish for a wonderful Christmas adventure!"

The next thing Gloria knew she was flying through the night. "On that dark planet you'll find the polka-dotted Pepperwills and the striped Valdoons," said her friend. "They have great need of Christmas magic."

She waved good-bye, and Gloria found herself slowly falling.

As Gloria passed through the clouds, she could see the walls that separated the lands of Valdoon and Pepperwill. In the woods between them she spotted the ruins of a castle.

Gloria landed among the striped soldiers. "It's a Pepperwill spy!" they cried. "Seize her!"

"I'm a friend," protested Gloria. "I've come to plan a Christmas celebration for the Valdoons and the Pepperwills."

"That's absurd!" cried the soldiers. "Ever since the castle blew up in the War of 1382, we Valdoons have hated the Pepperwills. Our feud will last forever!"

Across the valley Gloria was confronted by the Pepperwills. They repeated the story of the castle and the feud.

Like the Valdoons, the Pepperwills were not interested in Gloria's plans for Christmas. "We wouldn't dare leave our walls," they declared. "At any moment the Valdoons might attack."

These Pepperwills and Valdoons are almost as gloomy as goblins and witches, thought Gloria. She set off into the woods to explore the castle ruins.

If I rebuild this castle, it will cheer up the Valdoons and the Pepperwills, she thought. Then it will be the perfect spot for a Christmas celebration!

She set to work, but she soon realized that the job was too much for her. "I'll never be able to finish by Christmas," she said, sobbing.

That night she dreamed that her friend from
the storytelling circle came to comfort her.

As the dream ended, Gloria was awakened by the sound of tinkling bells and the arrival of elfin visitors. "We're from the North Pole," they explained. "We've come to help."

For the rest of the night the castle hummed and clattered with the sounds of construction.

Before leaving, one of the elves gave Gloria a recipe for a magic Christmas cake. "Mix these ingredients every day with love and generosity," he said. "By Christmas your cake will be irresistible!"

When the Valdoons and Pepperwills woke up, they were amazed to see the restored castle — and banners inviting everyone to a grand opening party.

Gloria waited all day for her guests to arrive. But no one came.

At sunset Gloria went to see the Valdoons. "Why didn't you come to my party?" she asked.

"Because you invited those horrid Pepperwills!" they declared.

On the Pepperwill side of the valley things weren't much brighter. "Celebrate with those dreadful Valdoons?" they cried. "NEVER! NEVER! NEVER! NEVER!"

Gloria thought for a minute. "All right," she announced. "Mondays, Wednesdays, and Fridays will be Pepperwill days at the castle."

The Pepperwills cheered.

Across the valley the Valdoons were equally delighted to hear the castle would be theirs on Tuesdays, Thursdays, and Saturdays.

Dividing the week between the enemies worked very well.

Everyone loved the way Gloria and the elves had rebuilt the castle, and as the days passed, it rang with the sounds of fun and frolic.

Before long both groups came to think of Gloria as a very special friend.

All this happiness drove away the gloomy clouds that had surrounded the planet for centuries. Soon the change was noticed by a band of patrolling witches. They swooped down to investigate.

Madame Pestilence was at the head of the formation. "So," she muttered, "our little Gloria is the culprit! We shall have our revenge!" A goblin spy was immediately sent to the castle.

Night after night the spy watched Gloria mixing and stirring the ingredients for her Christmas cake.

One Pepperwill morning in December Gloria bounced out of bed with a joyous whoop. She had thought of an idea to end the feud! Christmas was to be on a Sunday that year, and she announced a gala masquerade party at the castle.

The next day the Valdoons heard the same news.

However neither the Valdoons nor the Pepperwills were told that their enemies had also been invited.

The elves arrived to help everyone make costumes. Gloria baked dozens of cookies, pies, and puddings while she continued to work on her cake.

The smell of pastries and pine needles filled the air as gifts for friends were gleefully wrapped and labeled.

On Christmas Eve Gloria's cake was finally finished. "It's a masterpiece!" cried the elves. "Let's keep it hidden until after tomorrow's dinner, and then we'll have a grand presentation!"

Before going to bed they changed the labels on all the gifts so each Pepperwill present would seem to come from a Valdoon, and each gift for a Valdoon would seem to come from a Pepperwill.

Meanwhile the goblin spy had slipped out of the castle. He broomed toward the academy at top speed.

No sooner had the witches and goblins assembled and the spy's report been heard, than Madame Pestilence began pounding the great war gong. "Gloria's Christmas plot must be squelched immediately," she bellowed. "Here are your orders:

"ONE! Go to the castle and destroy Gloria's cake.

"TWO! Remain hidden under the cake cover until it is raised, and then CHARGE!

"THREE! Throw Gloria and the elves into the dungeon and chase the others back to their walls.

"GO AT ONCE!"

The attackers landed at the castle and quickly demolished the unguarded cake. From beneath the cover there came a muffled chorus of ooooohs, aaaaahs, and hmmmmms, followed by several hours of intense whispering.

Just before dawn, when all was quiet, Madame Pestilence slipped into the castle and hid behind the curtains.

On Christmas morning the costumed Pepperwills and Valdoons mingled and exchanged greetings without suspicion. Together they made their way through the falling snow and into Gloria's welcoming arms.

What a jolly time they had dancing, singing carols, and decorating the tree.

After the feast Gloria exclaimed, "Open your presents and take off your masks! MERRY CHRISTMAS TO ALL!"

The Valdoons and the Pepperwills were flabbergasted to discover that they had been celebrating and exchanging gifts with their enemies. "How did this happen?" they cried. "Are we under an evil spell?"

But there was no time for answers. A trumpet fanfare sounded and the elves cried, "Hear ye! Hear ye! We now present the great Christmas dessert."

Everyone gasped as the cake cover rose to reveal a pile of sleeping goblins and witches.

Madame Pestilence exploded from the curtains. "Wake up, you lazy louts!" she shrieked. "Remember your orders! Attack! Attack! Attack!"

The students awoke, but instead of obeying they hollered, "WE QUIT!"

Madame Pestilence was stunned. "You can't quit!" she roared. "It's forbidden! How dare you defy me?"

"Gloria's cake is to blame!" they cried. "It was *delicious!* We will never never NEVER eat creamed cockroach casserole again!"

Madame Pestilence flailed the air with her broom. "IDIOTS! BLOCKHEADS! TRAITORS!" she screamed. "I shall have my revenge!"

Thunder rumbled overhead, and the planet began to tremble. The Pepperwills and the Valdoons were paralyzed with fear.

Quickly the elves struck up a joyous Christmas carol. To everyone's amazement a shimmering star arched into the room and hovered above the tree. In the golden light the thundering and trembling ceased, and Madame Pestilence began to shrink.

For several moments her size and shape continued to change. "What's happening?" wailed the Pepperwills and Valdoons.

"She's becoming a cockroach!" exclaimed Gloria.

The witches and goblins cried, "We're free! We're free! Hooray for Gloria!"

All of this was too much for the Pepperwills and the Valdoons. They scrambled to escape from the castle and from one another.

Gloria hurried after her fleeing friends. "There is nothing to be afraid of!" she cried. "Don't go!"

"If the feud continues," warned the elves, "the planet will darken and Madame Pestilence will reappear."

The old enemies stopped and slowly turned around. "Please stay!" pleaded Gloria. "Remember how happy you were when the magic of Christmas entered your hearts?"

For several moments the Valdoons and Pepperwills stared at one another in silence. Then suddenly they felt ashamed of their long and bitter feud. "Our walls will come down," they said quietly. "And from this time onward we will be neighbors and friends in the united land of Pepperdoon."

All that night while the Christmas celebration continued, the planet of the Pepperdoons glowed more brilliantly than it ever had before.